The Secret of the Upstairs Room
and other ghostly tales

by

Gale Burnick

Watermill Press

Contents of this edition copyright © 1983 by Watermill
Press, Mahwah, New Jersey

All rights reserved. No part of this book may be used
or reproduced in any manner whatsoever without writ-
ten permission from the publisher.

Printed in the United States of America

Illustrations by James R. Odbert

ISBN 0-89375-820-5

Contents

Mother Love

"Please come, doctor. My baby's sick."

The young woman stood outside his door. She was very upset.

"Come inside a moment," Doctor Brown said.

"No, no," the woman said. "Please

come. It's the fever."

"Just wait then," the doctor said. "I'll get my bag."

Doctor Brown came back in a minute. The woman was gone. He looked up and down the street. It was night. He couldn't see very far. There was no one in sight.

I wonder what that was about, he said to himself. He shook his head and went back inside.

A few minutes later, the bell rang again. The same woman was at the door. Even in the dark, Doctor Brown thought she was very pale.

"Please, doctor," she said. "Please come see my baby."

"Why did you leave?" asked the doctor. "I only went to get my bag."

"Please come," the woman repeated. "I must get back to my baby." The woman

*Even in the dark, Doctor Brown thought
the woman was very pale.*

began to leave.

"All right," Doctor Brown said. "I'll come. But I must get my bag. Just wait. I'll only be a moment."

When the doctor returned, the woman was already down the street. He hurried to catch up with her.

"Miss!" Doctor Brown called. "Wait for me!"

The woman did not seem to hear him. She kept walking at a fast pace down the street. She reached the corner. There she turned to the right. By the time the doctor caught up, she was halfway down that block. They passed under a street light. The doctor again saw how pale the woman was.

"Are you O.K., Miss?" he asked.

The woman looked straight ahead. "It's my baby, Laura," she said. "You must help my baby."

They crossed the next street and kept walking.

"Where are we going?" Doctor Brown asked. "Where do you live?"

The woman didn't answer.

"Miss? Are you all right?" the doctor asked again.

"Laura's sick," she said. "My baby's sick."

"Have you been ill, too?" the doctor asked.

The woman said nothing more. The two had walked several blocks. They were nearing the cemetery. They reached the entrance. Suddenly, the woman turned and went in. Doctor Brown watched her go with surprise. After a moment, he turned to follow her.

"Miss? Where are you?" The doctor could no longer see her.

"Who's there?" someone asked. It was

Hank, the caretaker. He came up behind the doctor. "Oh, it's you, Doc," he said. "What brings you here this time of night?"

"A woman came to my door," said Doctor Brown. "She said her baby was very sick. She brought me here." The doctor looked around. "She came in here. Then I don't know. I didn't see which way she went."

"There shouldn't be anyone in here at night." Hank shook his head. "I only saw you come in. I didn't see any lady."

"I'll wait here a few minutes," the doctor said. "I'll see if she comes back."

The woman didn't come back to find the doctor. The next morning, Doctor Brown returned to the cemetery.

"Hank?"

"Hi, Doc." Hank was trimming the grass. He didn't stop as he spoke. "What

*The next morning, Doctor Brown returned
to the cemetery.*

can I do for you?"

"Did you see the woman after I left?" the doctor asked the caretaker. "Did she come back at all?"

"No," said Hank. "There was no one else all night."

The doctor stood a moment. "It puzzles me," he said. "She came to my door. She said her baby, Laura, had 'the fever.' Then she brought me here. She didn't look well herself."

"The fever, huh?" Hank said. "The fever was bad many years ago. There's a plot here just for those fever victims."

"Oh?" the doctor said. "Could you take me there?"

The two men went across the cemetery. The plot was on the far side. The graves were very old. The doctor read some of the stones. One caught his eye.

"This woman died a hundred years

ago," Doctor Brown said. "She died one hundred years ago yesterday — of yellow fever."

"This must be her baby then." Hank pointed to a small stone. It stood nearby. "The baby died one hundred years ago today."

Doctor Brown came over to see. "Well, I'll be," he said. He read the name on the stone out loud. "Laura."

Ralph

Jack knew the old farmhouse was haunted. He had heard stories about it since he was a child.

"Phooey," Jack said out loud. "Those stories are meant to scare children." There was no one else around, but Jack always felt better when he talked to himself.

A big storm was about to start. The wind was blowing and some rain was falling. Home was still a long way off. There was nowhere to go but the farmhouse.

"Why not?" asked Jack. He looked around first. There was no one in sight.

The sky had become very dark. The rain was falling harder. Jack climbed the steps to the farmhouse porch. Then he opened the door and went inside.

At first, he couldn't see much in the dark. Then his eyes got used to the dim light. He was in the dining room.

"This isn't so bad," Jack said.

An old table was in the center of the room. Several broken chairs were on the floor. One good chair stood near the table.

"There's nothing to be afraid of here," Jack said. "I guess I'll sit down." Jack

Jack climbed the steps to the farmhouse porch.

sat on the one good chair.

Outside, there was thunder and lightning. The rain came down harder and harder on the roof. When Jack looked at the doorway, he saw a cat. It was small and black.

"I see you came in out of the rain, too," said Jack. It was nice to have the cat for company.

The cat sat in the doorway. Jack still sat on the chair by the table. Then he thought he heard the door creak. When he looked at the doorway, he saw two cats. Both were black. The new one was bigger than the first. They stared at him.

"Hi, guys," Jack said.

The first cat looked at the second cat. "What do we do with him?" it asked.

"Wait for Ralph to come," the bigger cat said.

"Cats can't talk," said Jack. He waited, but the cats were quiet. "I must be hearing things. It must be the sound of the rain on the roof." Jack looked out the window at the rain. When he looked back, an even bigger black cat was there.

"Wow, three cats," said Jack.

The small cat looked at the big cat. "Do we do it?" it asked.

"Wait for Ralph to come," the big cat said.

Jack was getting scared now. "I heard you talk this time," he said. "It wasn't the rain."

The cats sat all in a row. They didn't move. They didn't say anything else.

"You know I'll leave as soon as the storm stops," Jack said to the cats. He was thinking about the stories he had heard. No one had ever told him who or what haunted this house. Could it be these strange cats?

"Oh, boy," sighed Jack. He hoped the storm would end soon. He looked back at the window. The storm seemed worse. Then he heard the door again.

"Oh, my!" said Jack. This cat was the size of a dog. And it was also black. It joined the other three. Jack looked at them, his eyes wide.

The first cat asked, "What do we do with him?"

"Wait for Ralph—no doubt about it," the new one said.

Jack got up. He walked back and forth on the dining-room floor. He was very worried now.

"Should I leave?" He said it more to himself than to the cats. "I can't leave yet, not in this rain," he told himself. "It's a long way home. The storm's too

*This cat was the size of a dog. It joined
the other three.*

bad." He kept walking back and forth. "They're just cats," he said.

The door flew open. Jack jumped at the sound. A black cat as big as a cow came in. Jack was afraid to move.

The cat as big as a cow looked at the others. "Now?" it asked.

"Let's wait for Ralph," the others said.

Jack ran to the window. He didn't want to know who or what Ralph was— not if Ralph was bigger than this last cat!

"Tell Ralph I can't wait!" Jack yelled. Then he jumped out of the window and ran home in the storm.

The Secret of the Upstairs Room

"You're such a know-it-all!"

"What's wrong with that?" asked Josh.

"You just think you know every-thing," said Bob. "You don't really."

"That room is *not* haunted," Josh said.

"I'll prove it to you." He was sorry as soon as he said that. What was he getting into now? But he decided to see it through all the way. "What do you want me to do?"

"Spend the night there." Bob looked smug. "No one's ever stayed the night in that room—not the *whole* night. I tell you, I'll never try it again!"

"O.K., I'll do it," said Josh. "Just tell me when."

"How about this Friday?" Bob said. "Start at 10:00 P.M. Stay until 6:00 A.M. Don't leave the room at all during those hours." Bob paused. "Get some sleep if you can."

"I'll be there," Josh said. He didn't know why he was doing this. But he was sure that the room wasn't haunted. He had said it to Bob. Now he had to prove it.

Friday night came too soon. Josh rode his bike over to Bob's house. It was a big, old house. It was probably a hundred years old. The more Josh thought about it, the more he wondered. Could it be haunted?

"It's on the third floor." Bob showed him upstairs. "It's the corner room. The other two rooms are for storage. This is supposed to be the guest room. It's got an unwelcome guest." Bob was edgy. He wished Josh luck and was gone.

The room seemed nice. It contained a bed and a chest of drawers. A blue rug was on the floor. By the windows was a desk. On the windows were light blue curtains. Built into one wall was a bookcase.

"At least I'll have something to read." Josh realized he was talking out loud to himself. "So what?" he said. He looked

It was a big, old house.

around the room again. Still he saw nothing strange. He decided to try and get some sleep.

He put on his pajamas and got into bed. He pulled the blanket up to his chin. The light was off. The room was very dark. He tried to relax.

Something tickled his toes!

Josh sat up in bed. He grabbed at his feet. There was nothing there. He was only imagining things. Slowly, he lay back down. This would be a long night.

Then, out of the corner of his eye, he saw a dark shape move!

Josh turned his head that way. At first, he saw nothing. Then there was movement. Josh laughed. It was the curtains he saw. They moved slowly in the breeze.

I'm scaring myself, Josh thought. *I'm imagining things. That's why people think they see ghosts. They tell scary stories until they believe in them. Then every little thing spooks them.* Josh relaxed now. *Well, I know better than that!* He shut his eyes. Soon he drifted off to sleep.

When he awakened, it was still dark. At first, Josh didn't know where he was. Then he remembered. He also heard what had awakened him.

A low moaning filled the room. The sound seemed to come from all around him. He listened to it. There was a loud rattle. It was clanking chains!

"I'm not imagining this!" he said softly.

The moaning went on. Now and again, the chains rattled.

What do I do now? Josh wondered. He didn't know, so he just waited.

After a while, the sounds stopped. Josh tried to stay awake. It didn't work.

Before long, he had dozed off.

Josh awoke in horror. He was in a madhouse. The moans and clankings were louder. They were the least of it. Now there was a crying sound. Then came banging and flapping. There were noises all around him!

"I'm getting out of here!" Josh cried.

He jumped out of bed. It seemed even darker in the room.

"Where did the door go?" Josh was in a panic. The sounds seemed to close in on him. "Where's the door?"

Alone in the dark, Josh felt like screaming. The light switch was by the door. He had to find the door! The rug seemed to tug at his feet. He rushed blindly across the room. His hands felt for the door.

"Ouch!" he cried as he ran into the wall. Josh felt his way along it.

He reached the bookcase in the wall. Josh ran his hands over it. A latch clicked, and the bookcase swung out from the wall. Beyond was a passageway. He saw a dim light at its end. Josh hurried to it. Something smashed into him.

"No, stop!" he yelled.

The crying and moaning were louder here. Something fluttered in his face.

"Help!" Josh called. But then his panic passed. Now he knew what had frightened him.

"*I've been a fool!*" he laughed. His eyes could see now in the dim light. "There are no ghosts! It's just this passageway!"

Josh looked around him. A missing shingle let a bit of moonlight in.

"That's the moaning." He touched the small hole. "The wind sounds like a moan when it blows in." Now he looked

"I've been a fool!" Josh laughed.

back down the passage. Two chains hung between the rafters. "That's what I first ran into. When the wind blows, the chains rattle."

Josh listened to the sounds around him. The crying came from up above. Josh looked up.

"And that's what flew into me— a pigeon. There's a nest of pigeons." Josh was grinning now despite the noise. "The wind and noises must bother the birds. So they cry and fly around. That must cause the flapping sounds."

Josh was feeling smug now. "This is like solving a puzzle," he said. Just then, the banging started again. It came from behind him.

"O.K.," he said. "What's this?" He went to see.

Above the missing shingle was one loose one. A gust of wind set it banging against the house.

"Well, I think that's all of it." Josh felt sure of himself now. "I *knew* that room wasn't haunted."

Josh returned to the guest room. He closed the bookcase door. The noises still echoed in the room. Now they didn't bother him.

"I am really tired now." Josh was yawning. He was asleep as soon as he got into bed.

"Josh? Are you O.K.?" It was Bob.

"Yes," said Josh, "I'm fine." He rose slowly. "What time is it?" The sun shone in through the blue curtains.

"It's 8:00," Bob said. "I hardly slept all night. I heard sounds from upstairs. I was sure you'd be coming down. When you didn't come out at dawn, I started to worry."

"I guess I was tired," said Josh. "I

slept very well."

Bob stared at him. "You slept *all* night?" he asked. He was amazed.

"Sure," said Josh. "After all, I *knew* this room wasn't haunted."

No More Complaints

"I can't stand it anymore!"

Jim Gordon threw his hands up in the air. He stopped walking back and forth. Then he sat down in a chair. Ruth, his wife, came over.

"I can't either," Ruth said. "But what

can we tell anyone? Can we say that the house is haunted? Even we don't really believe it."

"I don't believe it," Jim said. "But something is going on here. How do you explain it?"

"I can't," said Ruth. "We have doors that slam by themselves. We both know that doors don't slam by themselves." Ruth was upset. "But in our house, they do. That's not normal." Ruth sat down on the arm of Jim's chair. "Where did we get such a ghost?" she asked.

Matt Gordon walked into the room. He was Jim and Ruth's fifteen-year-old son. Matt came and sat down near his parents. "Maybe it's the ghost of a spoiled child. The kid's parents always told him, 'Don't slam the door.' Now that's all he wants to do."

"That's as good a story as any," said

35

Jim. "But that doesn't matter. I don't care what it is. I just want it to stop. And so does your mom."

Matt shrugged. "I do, too. But I don't know what to do about it. I'm not crazy about doors slamming all the time. It ruins my records." Matt stood up. "I don't have any ideas we haven't already tried. Sorry. I'm going up to sleep now. I'll see you two in the morning. Good night." He left and went upstairs to his room.

"Well," said Ruth, "what do we do?"

"I don't know," Jim said. "Maybe we should talk to someone else. Get some outside help. Maybe we can find some new ideas." He stood and began to pace the room. "We've tried everything we could. A door is open. It slams closed. No one is around. There is no wind blowing. So we close all the doors. This thing opens them and bangs them shut again. Isn't that terrific?"

"I know," said Ruth. "It's very upsetting." She was pacing the floor now, too. "Then we bolt the doors. So the bolts come out. Or the walls shake until we open the doors. What else can anyone try?"

"Let's find out," Jim said. "We can't go on like this. We need to do something. Tomorrow I'll call someone. We'll get help. We have to. Meanwhile, it's late. Let's go to sleep."

Ruth went upstairs. Jim turned out the lights. Then he went upstairs, too. Downstairs, the kitchen door slammed. Then the house was quiet.

"Dad?"

Matt stuck his head into his parents' room. He was whispering. "I heard something downstairs."

"It was just a door," his father said. "It was just another banging door. Go back to sleep, Matt."

"It wasn't a door," Matt said. He was still whispering. "I heard someone."

"All right," Jim said. He was awake now. "We'll go look." He was whispering, too.

Jim found a flashlight. Then he and Matt went down the stairs. Ruth followed them to the top of the stairs. She waited there in the dark.

"Hold it right there!" said a voice in the dark. Jim and Matt froze where they were. Then a man came out of their living room. He wore all black. He pointed a gun at father and son.

"Who's up there?" the man asked. He pointed up the stairs.

Jim answered, "It's just my wife."

"Have her come down the stairs," the

Jim and Matt went down the stairs.

gunman said. "And don't try any funny stuff."

"O.K.," said Jim. "We won't do anything." He looked at Matt. Then he called to Ruth. "Come on down, honey. It will be fine. Just come slowly."

Ruth did what Jim said. She joined Jim and Matt. The burglar moved the three into the living room. The only light was from the flashlight.

"Is there anyone else in the house?" the burglar asked.

"No one," said Ruth.

"Fine," the gunman said. He looked nervous. "I'm going to take a few things. Then I'll go. As long as you behave, no one will get hurt."

Just then, they heard a door slam. The Gordons knew it was their basement door. They knew no one was there. It was only their ghost.

The burglar didn't know that. "Who's that?" he asked.

"No one," Jim said. "A door blew shut."

The burglar looked doubtful—and nervous.

"Really," said Matt. "There's no one else here."

"We'll see," the gunman said. "You three stay here. Don't move. I'm going to check that door."

The burglar moved slowly out of the living room. He turned on the hallway light. He didn't see anything. His gun was still pointed at the Gordons. He went over to the basement door.

"Now don't move," the gunman said to the Gordons. "Don't do anything." He opened the basement door. He looked down the stairs. It was too dark to see down below. He looked back at the

The gunman looked back at the Gordons.

Gordons. They hadn't moved. Then the gunman went through the door. He went down the first two steps.

The door slammed closed! The burglar was shut in the basement. The Gordons heard him yell.

"Let me out!" he screamed. He tried the door but it wouldn't open. He rattled the doorknob. He banged on the door. It wouldn't open!

Jim, Ruth and Matt smiled at each other.

"Let's get out of here!" Jim said. The family hurried to the front door. They ran to their neighbors' house. Jim called the police from there.

When the police came, the burglar was still in the basement.

"Come out with your hands up!" The police had their guns drawn.

"I can't," the burglar said. "The door is

stuck." He rattled the knob. The door swung open. "Well, how about that?"

The police took the gunman out to their car. One officer stayed to talk to the Gordons.

"You folks were very lucky," the policeman said.

"Yes," said Ruth, "we know." She smiled at her husband and son. "We can't complain." Jim and Matt smiled back. None of them would ever complain again about their door-slamming ghost.

Spirit of the River

"It's lovely — and so big!"

"Are we really on a boat?"

Meg and Beth stepped into the Grand Salon.

"It's so different at night," Meg said. "There are lights everywhere. Look at how the mirrors reflect them."

"I'm looking at all the silver," said

Beth. "It shines so brightly. Oh, those velvet chairs and sofas look so soft."

The riverboat had been specially made. This was its first trip. Tonight was extra special. This was a costume ball.

The salon was full of people. They all wore old-fashioned clothes. Meg and Beth wore hoop skirts. They had made them themselves. Each hoped to win a costume prize.

"Imagine it's a hundred years ago," said Beth. "This is what riverboats must have been like. It's like stepping back through time."

Meg and Beth walked through the room. They said hello to other guests. Then they saw the group in the corner. One man was speaking. His hands moved as he spoke. He was big and had a full beard. He wore an old captain's

Meg and Beth wore hoop skirts.

outfit. Several people were listening to him.

The man was telling river tales.

"That was many winters ago. The river froze fast that year. The boats were caught by surprise. The ice pressed and squeezed. It destroyed many good boats.

"The *Marsha Valiant* was one." The man paused. "That was the first *Marsha Valiant*. I rebuilt her, though. This boat is the fourth to have that name."

The old captain looked up. "Well, I've told enough stories for now." He looked straight at Meg and Beth.

"I'm at your service, ladies." He tipped his cap and bowed slightly. "I am Jason Beauregard Smith, master of this vessel. My friends call me Captain Jay. Will you join me on the deck?"

Together, the three left the salon. On

the deck, Meg and Beth leaned over the rail. They looked out at the river.

"The river is a wonderful thing," said Captain Jay. "But it can fool you. At times, it makes you see things that aren't there. Then it won't let you see what you should. It's not easy to be a river pilot."

"Were you a pilot, Captain Jay?" Meg hoped to hear more river tales.

"I sure was." Captain Jay scratched at his beard. "I was raised on the river. I'm not like some of those fellows. Those city folks get some money and buy a boat. Then they think they own the river. They soon find out."

"Look at that rock!" Beth said, pointing. The *Marsha Valiant* passed close by a large rock sticking up in the middle of the river. "I didn't see it there a moment ago!"

The Marsha Valiant *passed close by a large rock sticking up in the middle of the river.*

Captain Jay grinned. "That's what I meant about the river. It can fool you. City folks don't realize that.

"It happened right here. That was some years ago. I was just the pilot on the *Marsha Valiant* then. A city fellow had bought a boat called the *Tribute*. The *Tribute* was a good boat, but too old to race. This fellow wouldn't take no for an answer. He wanted to race against the *Valiant*.

"That city captain said, 'Take the shortest way.' His young pilot did. But he didn't know the river well enough."

Captain Jay leaned on the rail. He looked back down the river.

"The river got them. It wrecked the *Tribute*. They drove the boat right into that rock we just passed. The other captain didn't see the rock until it was too late. It tore that boat apart."

51

Meg and Beth smiled at each other. They were enjoying the river and their companion. But that story! Did the captain expect them to believe that? What a tall tale!

"I'm sorry, ladies," Captain Jay apologized to them. "I didn't want to keep you from the party. I sometimes talk too much."

"Oh, we enjoyed it," said Meg. "Thank you."

"It's been my pleasure," said the captain. "I've got to go up to the wheel house now. It's time to check in with the pilot. You two have a nice time."

"Will we see you later?" asked Beth.

"Certainly." Captain Jay bowed to them. "You will see me later." He turned and left.

Meg turned to Beth. "How strange," she said. "He made me feel as if..."

"As if he were a *real* old-time captain?" Beth finished Meg's thought.

Meg took Beth's arm. "He does tell those tall tales well. Now, let's go inside. We're missing the party."

In the salon, a young man spoke. "It's time for the costume contest. The judges are among you. They will look over all the costumes. You won't know who they are—until later, that is. You might be standing next to one right now." The young man paused.

The people in the room looked around at one another. Each hoped to spot a judge.

"Look your best! Good luck!" the young man finished.

The girls moved about the large hall. At one end, they saw a sheet. It was hung across the wall.

"I wonder what that is?" Meg said.

"That's for after the costume prizes," answered the young man who had spoken earlier. He was standing behind them. "Are you ready to hear the winners? I'm about to announce them."

Beth squeezed Meg's hand. "I'm nervous. I hope one of us wins a prize."

The room grew quiet. The young man began to speak. He read off several winners.

"And for the most beautiful costume, we have a tie." The young man paused. "The winners are Beth Gold and Meg Lance."

Meg and Beth gasped. Then they rushed to get their prizes. Next, they stood to one side with the other winners.

The young man continued. "There's just one more thing tonight. Then the party goes on. Tonight we want to honor someone special.

"This is the fifth boat called *Marsha Valiant*. We chose that name because of the man who sailed the first four."

Meg nudged Beth. "He was wrong."

"Who?" asked Beth.

"Captain Jay. He said this was the fourth *Valiant*."

"Sssh," said Beth. "Let's hear."

They listened to the young man.

"We're honoring one of the finest river pilots. He piloted the first *Valiant* over one hundred years ago. He built three more. He was a great captain.

"We found a painting of that man. That picture has been restored. The new *Valiant* is where it will hang." The young man went to the sheet on the wall.

"Join with me now in viewing this painting—a portrait of the man whose spirit sails with us. Here is Jason Beauregard Smith." The young man

JASON BEAUREGARD SMITH

*The big, bearded man in the picture
was Captain Jay.*

lowered the sheet.

There was no doubt. The big, bearded man in the picture was Captain Jay.

Beth and Meg gasped. So did other people in the room. They had all seen him that night.

Meg spoke first. "Remember on the deck? You asked if we'd see him later."

"I know," said Beth quietly. "That was all he said. We would see him later."

The Test

"Do you want to join or not?"

"Yes, I do," said Liz, "but what do I have to do?" Liz stood outside her new high school. Two of her new friends were with her. They had been talking since school let out.

"We can't tell you now," said Barb.

Gwen nodded her head in agreement. "That's right," said Gwen. "It would spoil it." Gwen smiled at Liz. "Don't worry. The girls really want you to join our club. We all like you. What you'll have to do will be easy."

"When do I find out?" asked Liz. She still looked a bit uneasy.

"Can you meet us tonight?" Barb asked.

"I think so," said Liz.

"Well, meet us here at 9:00 tonight. Stand by the front door of the school." Barb looked around to make sure no one was listening. She continued. "Don't tell anyone where you're going. O.K.?"

"O.K.," said Liz. "I'll have to sneak out of the house, though. My parents wouldn't let me out so late. They would want to know where I was going."

"We'll see you later then," Gwen said.

The girls split up. Liz went straight home. It was almost time for dinner.

After dinner, Liz did her homework. About 8:00, she finished. She stood up and stretched. Then she spoke to her parents.

"I'm going upstairs now," Liz began. "I'm going to relax a bit. Then I'll be going to sleep. I'm very tired." She kissed her parents good night and went to her room.

In her room, Liz put on the radio. Then she got ready to go out. She put on old pants and a pair of sneakers. She found a poncho to wear over her clothes.

At 8:30, she pretended to go to sleep. She shut off the radio. Then she turned off the light. Quietly, she opened her window. Just outside was a large tree.

Liz went out the window and carefully lowered herself onto a strong tree branch. She climbed down to the ground. She hurried off toward the school.

Liz put on old pants and a pair of sneakers.

Liz stood in front of the school door. She heard a clock striking the time. Liz counted—it was 9:00. No one else was around.

Then Liz saw Gwen and Barb. "Hi," she called out to them.

"Hi," said Gwen. "We're glad you made it."

"So what now?" asked Liz. She was edgy.

"Just come with us," answered Barb.

"I don't suppose you'll tell me where," Liz said.

"That's right," said Barb, smiling.

The three girls set out. Barb and Gwen led Liz down one street after another. Finally, they reached the edge of town. There was a high fence in front of them. On the other side was the cemetery.

"Oh, boy," said Liz. "I think this must be it." She turned and faced her friends.

"It's not so bad," Gwen said. "You're not afraid of cemeteries, are you?"

"And we brought you a flashlight." Barb took it out of her back pocket as she spoke. She handed it to Liz.

Liz took the light. "I'm not afraid of cemeteries — at least not in the daytime. I've never been in one at night." She looked at Barb and Gwen. "What do I have to do?"

"It's easy," said Barb. She took a stick out of another pocket. It had a point at one end. "We want you to go into the cemetery. You'll have to find a grave there. We'll tell you which one. Put this stick in the grave, then you can go home. That's not hard, is it?" Barb gave the stick to Liz.

Gwen didn't wait for Liz to answer. "At sunrise, Barb and I will come and check. We'll make sure the stick is there.

That way, we'll know you did it at night."

"All I have to do is put the stick in?" Liz sounded unsure.

"Yes," said Gwen. "It won't hurt anything. Just remember you're not the first. All of us have had to do this. It's a secret we all share."

"You did the same thing?" Liz asked.

"Yes, last year," Gwen said.

"I did, too," said Barb.

"Then I guess there's nothing to it," Liz said. "Where do I go?"

Barb and Gwen took Liz to an opening in the fence.

"You can get in here," Barb said. "Go straight ahead until you find the main path. Follow that until you see a large column. It says 'Brown' on it. You can't miss it—not even at night. Right near it is a small column. It has a little statue on top. That's the grave. Put the stick in the ground. Then you're done. All right?"

"I think so," Liz said. "I might as well go do it."

"We'll see you at school tomorrow," Gwen said. She and Barb hugged Liz. Then the two left.

Liz went through the fence. She held the stick in one hand. The flashlight was in the other. It seemed even darker inside the cemetery. Liz turned on the light. It lit the way in front of her. It also made strange shadows.

Liz found the main path. Gravel crunched under her feet. In the dark, every noise sounded louder. Liz had never felt so alone.

Ahead, Liz saw the large column. "Thank goodness!" she whispered. When she reached it, she left the path. She flashed the light around. She looked for the small column.

"Where is it?" Liz said. She was getting scared. It was too dark, too quiet. Liz thought she saw shapes behind every gravestone. Finally, she saw the small column. The little stone statue sat on top of it.

Liz went over to it. She stood there, looking down. She began talking to herself. *I'll just do it and get it over with.*

Liz got the stick ready. She held it out, point down. Liz bent over. Then she closed her eyes. She pushed the stick into the ground. As she did, she felt someone grab her poncho.

"No, please!" she cried. She tried to get free. She was afraid to open her eyes. "Please, let me go!"

Liz pulled herself free from the poncho. Then she stood, opened her eyes, and began to run.

As she reached the main path, Liz

tripped. The flashlight fell from her hand. She left it and kept running. She ran all the way down the main path. She didn't stop to find the hole in the fence. She climbed right over it.

Then Liz started running toward home. She didn't stop even long enough to look behind her. She ran all the way. When she reached her house, Liz banged on the door. Soon her parents came and let her in.

The next day at school, Gwen and Barb looked for Liz. She didn't show up in class.

"Do you think something happened?" Gwen asked.

"I don't know," Barb said. "Maybe Liz's parents found out."

"They wouldn't have kept Liz out of school, though," said Gwen.

By lunch break, Gwen and Barb were

Liz left the flashlight and kept running.

getting worried.

"Let's skip lunch and go to the cemetery," Barb said.

"Yeah," Gwen agreed. "We should have done that earlier the way we said we would."

The two girls walked there quickly. They slipped in through the fence. Then they followed the main path. They soon came to the large column.

"There's the flashlight!" said Barb. She pointed at the ground.

"Something must have happened," Gwen said.

Gwen and Barb looked at each other. Now they were getting scared. They held hands as they walked toward the small column. They didn't know what to expect.

On the grave was Liz's poncho. The stick was pushed through one edge of it.

"Gosh," said Gwen. "Liz must have scared herself silly. She stuck the stick through her poncho. In the dark, she couldn't see that. She must have thought someone grabbed her."

Gwen bent down and pulled the stick out. Then she picked up the poncho.

"We'd better go see Liz," said Barb. "We'll tell her what happened. And we'll tell her how sorry we are. I hope she'll still be our friend."

The White House Ghost

"We're in trouble now," said Ann.

"You're telling me!" Judy said.

Their parents were nowhere in sight. Neither was the rest of the White House tour group. The two girls were alone in the hallway.

"We only went into that room for a

minute," Ann said. "And now the whole group is gone."

"We shouldn't have done that," replied her sister. "But I did want to look at that chair. I just love rocking chairs."

"Well, now what do we do?" said Ann. "Which way should we go? Mom and Dad are going to be so mad at us."

The girls were on the second floor of the White House. They had gone into one of the rooms while their special tour group stopped in the hall outside.

"They were looking at that painting," said Judy. "But they could have gone anywhere."

"May I help you?"

The girls jumped. An old man had come up behind them.

"Are you looking for someone?" he asked.

"Er, yes," Ann said. "We, uh, got lost.

72

We were with our parents on the White House tour."

"It was my fault," said Judy. "We saw that small room. I wanted to see the rocking chair in there. We only took a minute."

"But everyone is gone," Ann continued. "We don't know where they went."

"I think I can help you," the old man said.

"Do you work here?" asked Ann. The old man had a feather duster under his arm.

"You might say that," he answered. He held out his hand to the girls. "I'm Jerry," he said.

"I'm Judy and this is my sister, Ann." They shook his hand.

"Has your group been to the East Room yet?" Jerry asked.

"No," said Judy.

*The old man had a feather duster
under his arm.*

"Well, let's go there then," Jerry said. "Every group goes there sometime. We'll catch up with them."

Jerry led them off down the hallway. He moved slowly. Here and there, he stopped. He'd do some dusting with his feather duster. He dusted some paintings, a chair, and a vase. Then they went down a flight of stairs.

"This is called the State Floor," Jerry said. He stopped to dust a painting. "A lot of fancy things go on here. The East Room is over there." Jerry pointed to their left.

"It's so big," said Judy, looking in.

"And nobody's in there," Ann said.

"You go on in and wait," said Jerry. "I'm sure they'll be along soon."

Jerry was dusting the door now. The girls went slowly into the room.

Ann turned back to the door. "Thank

you...," she began. "Jerry?" Ann looked back toward Judy. "He's gone," she said.

"He couldn't have gone far," said Judy. She headed for the door. "We should say thank you."

"We're not leaving this room," Ann said. "We'll get lost again."

"I suppose you're right," Judy agreed. "Let's just look around this room."

The girls were in front of the big portrait of George Washington. They heard the group coming from the hall.

"And ahead of us is the East Room," the guide said. "It's the largest room in the White House."

Their parents saw them right away. "Where have you been?" both said at once.

"We got lost," Judy said.

"But this old man brought us here," Ann continued. "He knew the tour would come here."

Their parents looked at them. "We'll talk about this later," their mother said.

"I'll tell the guide we found you," said their father.

The girls looked down at their feet.

"We're sorry," said Judy.

"Let's hear the rest of the tour," said their mother.

They joined the girls' father near the guide. The guide was still talking about the East Room.

"President and Mrs. Adams were the first to live in the White House," he said. "Mrs. Adams used to hang her wash to dry in this room. Some people have seen her ghost in here."

"Is she the only White House ghost?" asked one woman.

"Oh, no," said the guide. "There are several. Abe Lincoln is one. So are

The girls looked down at their feet.
"We're sorry," said Judy.

Thomas Jefferson and Andrew Jackson. Dolly Madison's been seen in the garden. In fact, there's even an old janitor who walks the halls. He carries his feather duster with him."

Ann and Judy looked at each other. "Do you think...?" Judy said.

The guide was moving toward the door. "Let's go down and see the kitchen now," he said.

The group went down to the ground floor. Ann and Judy stayed near their parents. They waited for a chance to talk to the guide. On the way out of the kitchen, the guide walked near them.

"Excuse me," Ann said. "We were curious. Does the ghost with the feather duster have a name?"

"Hmmm, let me think," said the guide. "Yes, he does. It's Smith, Jerry Smith."

The Last Time I Saw Aunt Flo

"The party's about to start."

My brother, Alan, called from inside the house. I was on the porch in the back looking at the beach. Where was Aunt Flo? I decided I had better go in.

"Happy Birthday!" everyone yelled.

*I was on the porch in the back looking
at the beach.*

I tried to look pleased, and really, I was. My friends were all here. So was my family, except for Aunt Flo. She had never missed my birthday before. She lived in a small house. It was just two miles up the beach. It was the first place I went when I learned how to walk. I always loved her stories. I also enjoyed the cookies she would bake me.

"Hope!" My mother was calling me from the kitchen. "When do you want to open your presents? You could wait until after we eat." She was busy fixing the food.

"Mom, Aunt Flo isn't here," I said.

She looked up from the counter. "I'm sorry, Hope," she said. "I've been so busy. I forgot to tell you Aunt Flo is sick. She can't come today. What about your presents?"

"I guess after the food, but before the

cake," I said. I felt bad. I went back to the party and tried to be cheerful.

Alan put on records and I danced with my friends. Then we ate. I was feeling much better. We all sat in the living room while I opened my presents. Everyone was having a good time.

I couldn't forget Aunt Flo, though. She had made me feel special ever since I was a child. Her mother's name had been Hope. She told me that was why I was her special niece. Her mother had been very pretty. As I grew older, Aunt Flo told me I looked more and more like her mother.

"Wake up, sleepy," Alan said. "It's time for the cake."

I guess I had been daydreaming. My mom brought the cake in, and my dad lit the candles. I blew them all out. My wish was for Aunt Flo to be with me on every birthday.

After having some cake, I went out on the porch. The tide was out. I could see a long way up the beach. Someone was headed my way. After a few minutes, I could see who it was.

"Aunt Flo! Aunt Flo!" I ran out along the beach to greet her.

"Happy Birthday, Hope! You look more lovely all the time!"

"Mom said you were sick. I was afraid you'd miss my birthday."

"Oh, don't worry about me, child. I had to bring you your present, didn't I?" Aunt Flo smiled. She took a ring off her finger. She handed it to me. The ring was gold with a pearl in the center. There were small diamonds around the pearl. They were bright in the sun.

"This was my mother's," Aunt Flo said. "See, it says 'Hope' inside." She

"This was my mother's ring," Aunt Flo said.

showed me the old writing inside the ring. "Come on now, take it. It's yours."

"Oh, Aunt Flo..." I didn't know what to say.

"It's yours and that's final." She slipped it on my finger.

Just then, I heard Alan calling. He was waving at me to come back.

"Come on, Aunt Flo," I said. "Let's go. The party's still going on. Everyone will be glad to see you."

"You go on ahead, Hope," she said. "You can show them all your present."

I was so happy and excited that I agreed. I ran back to the house. When I came in from the porch, everyone was quiet. I knew something was wrong. My parents came over and hugged me. Then Mom told me to sit down.

"Hope, I have bad news. Aunt Flo is dead."

"She can't be!" I cried. I felt the ring on my finger. I looked out at the beach, but no one was there.

"It's true," Dad said. "We got the phone call a few minutes ago."

I started to say more, but stopped. I thought about my birthday wish. It must have come true. I was crying, but I smiled. I knew now that I'd see Aunt Flo every year.

The White Riders

"May I share your fire, mister?"

The cowboy rode up quietly. Old Bill was nearly asleep by the fire. He didn't show his surprise. He looked up at the stranger. It was a dark night. All he could see was a lone man on horseback. Old Bill looked back at the fire.

"I guess so," he replied.

The newcomer got off his horse. He tied it to a nearby tree.

"It's very dark tonight," he said. He sat down by the fire. "Do you work around here?" he asked.

"Yes," Old Bill said, "I have for years now." Old Bill took a pipe from his pocket. He filled it with tobacco. "I've been checking the fences for a few days. There's a lot of fences, so there's a lot of mending to be done." Old Bill lit his pipe.

"What about you?" he asked. He tried to get a good look at the stranger. There was only the light of the fire. The cowboy was hard to see in its glow.

"Me? I'm just passing through," the cowboy said. He sighed. "I'm always on the way from one place to another."

"Did you see any riders out there?" Old Bill asked. He took the pipe out of

*Old Bill took the pipe out of his mouth
and pointed with it.*

his mouth and pointed with it. "I'm sure I heard riders. It was just after sundown. It sounded like a dozen horses riding by. They sounded close. I didn't see anyone, though."

"Maybe they were White Riders," the cowboy said.

Old Bill puffed on his pipe. "I don't know of any White Riders."

"They're not from around here," said the cowboy. "They come and go wherever they are needed." He settled down some more by the fire.

"There are eleven men, dressed all in white. They ride white horses. They have silver spurs and stirrups, too." The cowboy paused. "They have one extra horse, with no rider. It's a white horse. On it is another white outfit — hat, shirt, boots, everything. It's all rolled up, hat on top, tied to the saddle."

Now the stranger was looking right at Old Bill. "They ride through the night," he said, "always looking. They're looking for the next one to ride away with them. That person is the one who will ride the riderless horse."

The stranger shifted again. He looked into the fire. "When people hear the White Riders, they lock their doors. They don't want the White Riders to stop. Where they stop, someone has died. They come to claim the body. They come only at night, though. They're never seen by day."

The cowboy paused again. "Your pipe's gone out, old timer."

Old Bill looked at his pipe. It was still in his mouth. He struck a match on his boot and relit it.

"Don't you get lonesome just traveling all the time?" Old Bill asked.

"How about you?" asked the stranger. "Don't *you* get lonesome? You spend so many days and nights out here. Wouldn't you rather be at home?"

"I used to," said Old Bill. Smoke rose from his pipe as he talked. "Years ago, I used to get lonesome. I'd miss my family. But I ran this ranch for them. I wanted them to have good things. Time changed that. First it was my little girl."

Old Bill puffed on his pipe. "She was about eight or nine. She was very pretty. Her horse threw her one day. She hit her head on a rock. She never woke up."

Old Bill stared into the fire for a while. Then he went on. "Then there was my boy. I was so proud of him. He helped me run the ranch. He did a good job. It was all going to be his some day. But when he was seventeen, the fever came. A lot of people became sick. Many died.

My son was one of the first to go. After that, my wife and I kept on. It was never the same, though."

His pipe had gone out again. Old Bill still kept it in his mouth. "Some years ago, my wife passed on. I don't know why I still work this place. It really doesn't matter now where I am. I can be out here or back at the house. My memories are all I have. And I have them with me wherever I am."

The two men had been talking for some time. The fire was dying out.

"We should turn in for the night," Old Bill said. He spread out his gear near the fire. The stranger did the same.

There was a dim gray light before sunrise. Old Bill awoke. He heard horses riding into the camp. He knew what he would see when he opened his eyes. He opened them.

The stranger was dressed all in white.

The stranger was already up. He was dressed all in white. He rode a white horse with silver stirrups. Ten other White Riders were with him. They led a riderless horse.

"I guess that one is for me," Old Bill said. The stranger nodded yes.

Old Bill went to the horse. He undid the roll on the saddle. Quickly, he changed into the white outfit. Dawn was near. They would have to be on their way before day began.